GRUNT AND THE GROUCH

Freaky Funfair!

FOR
MARJORIE & STEPHEN
(WHO ARE NOTHING
LIKE THE TROLLS!).
LOVE, T.C. x

STRIPES PUBLISHING
An imprint of Magi Publications
1 The Coda Centre, 189 Munster Road,
London SW6 6AW

A paperback original
First published in
Great Britain in 2011.

ISBN: 978-1-84715-161-2

A CIP catalogue record for
this book is available from
the British Library.

2 4 6 8 10 9 7 5 3 1

Printed and bound
in the UK.

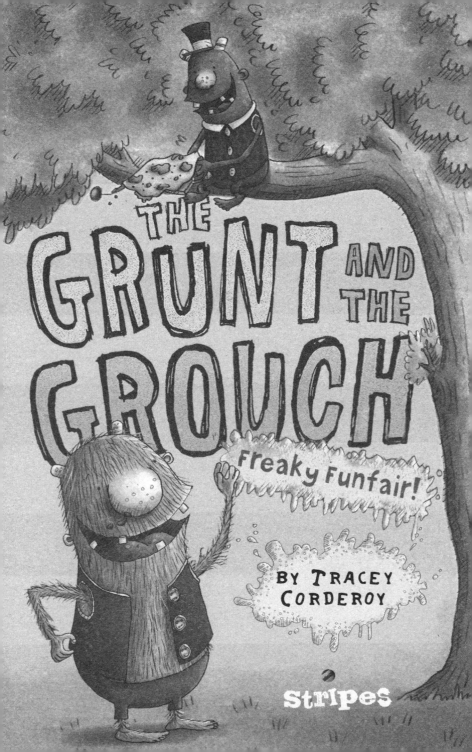

THE GRUNT AND THE GROUCH

Freaky Funfair!

BY TRACEY CORDEROY

Stripes

CONTENTS

CHAPTER ONE

Rippp! The Grouch tore open the last box of Honey Hearts and shoved his small green hand inside. This had to be the one – it *had* to be!

"Well?" asked Grunty. "Is it in there?"

"Hang on," said Grouchy. "Keep your hair on!"

He searched through the sickly-sweet cereal for the little bumper car that would win them a free trip to Wizzy World, the wickedest theme park *ever*!

"*Well?*" cried Grunty impatiently.

"Wait!" said Grouchy. "There *might* be something right … at … the … bottom."

He tipped the cereal on to the floor and quickly sifted through it, but there wasn't a single bumper car in sight.

"Bah! I *told* you!" growled The Grunt. "And now we've spent all our money on *revolting* Honey Hearts when we could've bought yummy Coco Snots or Lice Krispies."

Just then, Grunty's tummy rumbled. "Did you hear that?" he groaned. "I'm starving! But all we've got is … *these*."

He scooped up a handful of Honey Hearts and stuffed them into his mouth. The sweet little hearts fizzled on his tongue and he shuddered.

"Sorry," sniffed Grouchy miserably. For a few moments nobody spoke. Then, suddenly…

"OWWW!"

A fountain of sticky cereal shot out of Grunty's mouth, along with a bit of broken tooth AND…

Look, Grunty! You've found a bumper car!

"Huh?" muttered Grunty. "But … that means … *we've won!*"

He snatched up an empty cereal box and read through the prize-winners' instructions. "Look, Wizzy World trains leave every hour. Let's go!"

He refilled the empty cereal box with a pile of Honey Hearts. "We'll take these in case we're *starving* on the train," he said.

"And these!" beamed Grouchy, tossing over a jar of bogeys and a bottle of pond water off the goodies shelf. "Ready, steady – race you there!"

They zoomed out of the house and didn't stop until they reached the station. A Wizzy World train was just about to leave.

"Quick!" cried Grunty, hopping aboard and diving into the "quiet" carriage.

"I'm right behind you!" Grouchy puffed.

They zipped along the aisle and plonked themselves down in two empty seats. "*Yippee!*" cheered the trolls. "We made it!"

The lady peep-squeak across the table stared at them. She'd never seen anything quite so revolting!

Nervously, she fingered her strings of pearls, and pulled her daughter closer.

The stationmaster blew his whistle and the train chuffed away down the track. "Hey, Grouchy, fancy a sing-song?" yelled Grunty. "I know tons of train songs."

"OK!" giggled Grouchy. "*Trollific!*"

For the next hour they belted out songs (none of which were in tune).

Finally, the lady opposite could bear it no longer. "W-would you like a pear drop?" she asked, hoping it would shut them up.

"Who, *us*?" muttered Grunty. "Well … um … thanks!"

"And *you* can have some Honey Hearts," beamed Grouchy. "It's only fair!"

He grabbed the box of Honey Hearts and emptied it into Mrs Posh Pearls' handbag. Then Grunty chucked in some bogey sprinkles and the pond water.

"*N-no!*" cried Mrs Posh Pearls as he slopped it back towards her.

"It's OK," said Grunty, swiping her pear drops. "There's no need to say thanks!"

CHAPTER TWO

Ten minutes later, the train hissed to a stop. "HOORAY!" cheered the trolls. "We're here!"

They raced down the aisle, flung open the door and hurried out on to the platform.

"Right," said Grunty. "Which way now?"

"This way, darling," sniffed Mrs Posh Pearls, as she led her daughter past the trolls. "Through that door then it's only a short walk to Wizzy World."

On hearing this, Grunty caught them up. "We'll walk with you!" he said.

"Good idea," cried Grouchy, pattering over.

They headed off. "This is nice," said The Grouch, nudging Mrs Posh Pearls. "Hey, did you find a winning bumper car?"

"Er … no!" Mrs Posh Pearls snapped. "Though Pansy ate *thousands* of Honey Hearts."

"*Unlucky!*" Grouchy tutted. "We did!" He stuffed a hand under his hat and pulled out the little bumper car. "See?" he said. Pansy glared at him.

They walked on, Pansy still glaring and Mrs Posh Pearls pink with rage. Five minutes later, they reached the queue for Wizzy World.

"Well then," sniffed Grunty, "see you later!" Mrs Posh Pearls looked confused.

"Honey Hearts winners don't have to queue for a thing," explained Grouchy.

He fumbled under his hat again and pulled out what looked like a used-before sick bag! Pansy clapped a hand to her mouth.

"Here!" he said, handing it to her. "In case any rides make you sick!"

"We'll have it back on the way home," nodded Grunty. "We'll save you a seat on the train."

"Remember, fill it *right* to the top!" sniggered Grouchy.

GRUNT AND THE GROUCH

With that, the trolls marched up to
the gates where a lady stood waiting for
Honey Hearts winners.

Her head was buried in a Wizzy World
guide as she began her usual speech.
"Welcome. Let the fun begin. All food
and rides are free to you lucky er—"

"*Trolls!*" squeaked Grouchy excitedly.
The peep-squeak lady glanced up.

"Aaargh!" she screamed at the sight
of their filthy faces. Quickly, she
passed them two rosettes. "You'll
need to wear
these," she
gulped. "And
here are some
nice ... *clean*
maps."

The trolls slapped on their rosettes and darted inside. "Right!" Grunty grinned. "What shall we go on first?"

He opened his map. "Hmmm…" he said. "Rocket Blast-Off sounds good."

"*What?*" gasped Grouchy. "But I don't know how to drive a *rocket*!"

He glanced around. "Oooh, look! I might try that Wee Jolly Chums ride."

Grunty glowered. "No *way*! It's for *babies*!"

"But only if you go on with me," continued Grouchy. "*Please!* Then *you* can choose."

"OK, OK!" Grunty sighed. "Come on!"

When all the children (and the trolls!) were safely aboard, some tinkly music sounded and the ride began.

Several peep-squeaks tittered at
Grunty riding Polly the Pink Flamingo,
whilst Grouchy sat inside Ben the Bus,
quivering.

"S-slower!" he shrieked, as the ride
crawled around slower than a sleepy snail.

Grunty shook his head. "What a *wimp*!"

Finally, the music stopped and it was
time to get off. "Right!" cried Grunty. "*My*
turn to choose. Now, let me see…"

CHAPTER THREE

Grunty looked at his map then marched off towards the Mirror Maze. "N-nothing too s-s-scary," Grouchy called.

"As if!" Grunty grinned. "Follow me!"

On they walked, past the Teacup Twirl … past the Raging Rapids … past the Spooky Shack (which looked a bit like home!). Finally, "Look!" cried Grunty. "Check *these* out!"

Grouchy gulped. "N-not the Bumper Cars. I don't know how to drive a c-car!"

"You managed fine on Ben the Bus," growled Grunty.

Suddenly, a horn sounded and a group of pushy peep-squeaks raced towards the waiting cars.

"Oi!" boomed Grunty. "Not so fast!" Everyone froze and gaped at the huge purple troll. "*We* get first pick," he nodded, tapping his rosette.

He plonked Grouchy into a red car and dived into a blue one. Nervous-looking peep-squeaks then hurried to the rest.

Baaap! Another horn sounded and the cars started zipping about. All except for one...

"Watch out!" shrieked The Grouch, as a flashy green car went rocketing past. If only he could get to a nice, quiet spot.

He grabbed hold of the steering wheel. "Now what?" Grouchy muttered to himself. He needed to turn so he stuck out an arm and signalled.

"Hey, Grouchy!" laughed Grunty, zooming by. "You're meant to *bump* not *signal*! Here, watch me..."

He rammed into the back of another car. The driver spun round. "Aaargh!" screamed Mrs Posh Pearls. "*You!*"

GRUNT AND THE GROUCH

"Fancy bumping into you!" cried
Grunty, giving her a wave. "Now, let me
see…" He peered around. "Who's next?"

Revving his engine, he hurtled away,
bashing every car in sight. One by one,
they spun off to the sides.

Finally, there was only one car that Grunty hadn't bumped. "Oi, Grouchy!" snorted Grunty. "I'm coming to get you!"

He spun the car round and headed straight for him. "No!" Grouchy gulped. "I … I … *that's not funny!*"

He tootled off as fast as he dared, but Grunty was right on his tail.

"*Gotcha!*" he cried, as his car walloped Grouchy's. *Doof!*

"*Aaargh!*" yelled The Grouch, as he flew from his car and sailed over a queue of peep-squeaks. He landed on the roof of a candyfloss stall. "Grunty! Grunty! Help!" he squeaked. "I'm stuck!"

Grunty raced to the rescue. "Hee, hee!" he chuckled, lifting Grouchy down. "Wasn't that fun? Fancy a go on the Ghost Train next?"

"No!" gasped Grouchy. "I'm – er – *hungry*. And grub's free for us winners, remember?"

"Oh yeah!" Grunty grinned. "In that case, let's get scoffing!"

In no time at all, their tummies were crammed with candyfloss, popcorn, burgers in buns and Wizzy World hot dogs with red-sauce-and-brown-sauce- and-lashings-of-thick-yellow-mustard.

"Right," said Grunty with a burp. "Shall we go on a few more rides?"

"If we have to," groaned Grouchy, rubbing his tummy.

They each took turns to choose rides, but Grouchy didn't get any braver. He screamed like a baby on the Dino Dippers. He shook in the Spooky Shack. And he hid under his seat on the Runaway Train!

Finally, Grunty had had enough of his scaredy-cat ways. "Stop being such a wimp!" he growled. "The next ride's the best of all." He pointed towards it. Grouchy squeaked in terror.

"C'mon!" Grunty nodded. "Time for the Loop the Loop!"

CHAPTER FOUR

Grunty hurried over to the roller coaster, with Grouchy pattering behind. No way was he was going on the Loop the Loop! He needed an excuse, and fast.

Then he spied it. *A measuring post!* Grouchy grinned to himself. With a bit of luck he'd be too small to ride!

They made their way to the front of the queue, and Grouchy let out a wail. "Oh no! A measuring post. I'm *way* too small for that ride. They'll *never* let me on! Ah, well."

He turned to leave.

"Not so fast," growled Grunty. He scooped him up, thumped over to the post and plonked him down beside it.

"OK," yawned the measuring-man. "Stand up tall."

The Grouch pretended to do as he was told, but when no one was looking, he bent his knees a bit. "Too short!" sniffed the measuring-man. "NEXT!"

"*Really?*" beamed Grouchy, springing up and bashing his head on the TALL ENOUGH arrow.

"*Wait!*" cried Grunty. "He's just grown a bit. Look!"

Grouchy crouched down, but it was too late. "*Fine,*" sighed the measuring-man. "On you go…"

Grunty clapped his hands excitedly. This was going to be great!

"I-I … need the toilet," muttered Grouchy.

"No you don't!" cried Grunty. He grabbed Grouchy's arm, dragged him up some steps and into an empty car. An attendant hurried over and strapped them in.

"Don't look so scared!" laughed Grunty. "It's only a titchy roller coaster!"

"No it's not," sniffed Grouchy. "It's a *monster*."

Just then, a siren sounded and their car swished off. "Grunty," said Grouchy. "Can I sit on your lap?"

"No!" snorted Grunty. "Stop being such a baby!"

A few seconds later, they picked up speed then glided around the first bend. "Too fast!" gulped Grouchy.

"FASTER!" boomed The Grunt.

Next, they went over some gentle bumps. "Woohoo!" cried Grunty excitedly. "I think we're about to go up!"

"What?" gasped Grouchy. "Up? *Oh no!*"
Their car started to climb a steep
track. "NOOOO!" wailed Grouchy,
covering his eyes.

We're dooooomed!

As they reached
the *very* top ... the car
... ground ... to a ...
halt. Grouchy could hear
the wind whistling by.
"G-Grunty," he said
shakily. "I really do need the
loo!" There was no reply.
What was going on?

Grouchy peeped through his fingers, a tiny bit at first. Then a tiny bit more. Actually, it wasn't too bad up here!

He lowered his hands and looked around. The view was *trollific*! Grouchy could see the whole wide world.

Whoopee!

Reaching out, he tried to catch a cloud. Then he waved to the peep-squeaks below. "Grunty!" he giggled. "Isn't this cool?" He nudged him. "Hey, Grunty … *what's wrong?*"

The Grunt was gripping the side of the car. "Keep still!" he squeaked, his eyes tight shut. Then suddenly…

WHHHOOOOSSSSSSHHHH!

Down they went, faster and faster,
hurtling towards the loop the loop.

"HELP!" screamed Grunty as they
tumbled and twirled.

"Whoopee!" cheered Grouchy.

"This is the BEEESSSST!"

Help!

The rest of the ride whizzed by in a whirlwind of bends and drops. Grouchy had never had such fun (and Grunty had never been so quiet!).

Finally, when they glided to a halt, Grunty shot out of his seat and staggered down the steps.

"Now who's being a baby?" Grouchy giggled.

"I wasn't s-scared," gasped Grunty. "I was just, um … *pretending* … to make you feel better!"

"Oh!" tittered Grouchy. "Well, it worked! Hey, let's go on again. I loved touching the clouds!"

Grunty peered up. "NO WAY!"

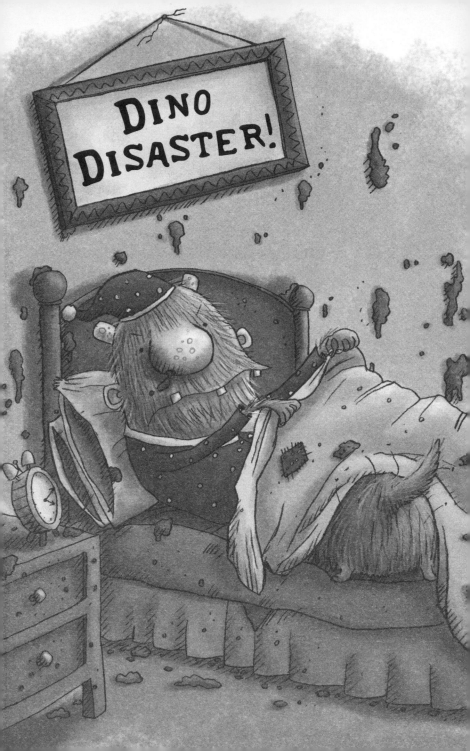

CHAPTER ONE

Rustle, rustle!

Grunty woke with a snort. There was something in his bed! Something *hairy*. Nervously, he reached out a foot and gave it a tiny poke. *Sniff! Sniff!* went the something, noisily.

"Hang on a minute!" growled The Grunt. He lifted the blankets and peered in. Two big eyes blinked back…

"GROTBAG!"

The fleabaggy dog licked Grunty's

nose then started pawing the mattress. "Nooo," groaned Grunty, throwing back the covers. "It's still night time. Shoo!"

He chucked his pillow at The Grouch and it hit him – *thunk!* – in the face.

"N-nightmare!" gasped Grouchy, waking in panic.

Troll-eating pillows!

"Never mind *that*!" cried Grunty.
"Something's wrong with Grotbag. Look!"

The Grouch raced over and
gaped at Grotbag, now
digging a hole in Grunty's
mattress. "Maybe he's
playing pirates?" he said.
"Digging for doggy treasure?"

"*What?*" boomed Grunty.
"Don't be so ridiculous!"

He got out of bed, scooped up the
dog and thundered downstairs.

"Or perhaps he's lonely?" called
Grouchy, pattering behind.

Ignoring him, Grunty marched into
the sitting room and plonked Grotbag
into his basket. "Stay!" he bellowed.
But Grotbag just howled in reply.

He waited for Grunty to turn away, then jumped back out again and started sniffing everything in sight.

"What's he doing NOW?" roared The Grunt.

Grouchy shrugged. "I think he's *looking* for something," he said. "Maybe we could help him find it?"

"Fine!" snapped Grunty. "Anything for a bit of PEACE AND QUIET!"

Grouchy thought for a moment. "OK," he said, "let's collect up all Grotbag's favourite things and show them to him one by one. He's *bound* to wag his tail when he sees what he's looking for."

Grunty gave a sigh. "I hope you're right."

Five minutes later, they were ready.
"I'll go first!" Grouchy smiled and held up
a lump of gooey earwax. Grotbag
blinked, hung his head and whimpered.

"Right, my turn!" cried The Grunt. He
whipped off a whiffy bedsock and wafted
it through the air. Grotbag gave
it a tiny sniff … and
sighed.

Bit by bit, the floor became littered with Grotbag's favourite things, but his big, bushy tail didn't wag once.

"I give up," grumbled Grunty. "We've tried *everything.*"

"Hang on!" cried Grouchy. "We've forgotten his bone! I bet *that's* what he's looking for."

He looked at Grotbag. "Bone?" he said. Grotbag stared back miserably. "How can I make you *understand*? Oh, *wait*," said Grouchy, "I know!"

He bared
his teeth, flew
at Grunty's leg,
and started to
gnaw like mad.
"OWW!" wailed
Grunty. "What are
you *doing*?"

He prized off the tiny troll
and dumped him on the floor,
but Grouchy leaped back up
again. "LOOK!" he cried.
"Grunty, look at Grotbag!"

Grotbag's tail was
wagging like mad, and his
bark was bright and happy.
"See!" beamed Grouchy.
"He *has* lost his bone!"

43

"Oh no," groaned Grunty. "That means we've got to *find* it!"

The trolls got dressed, gulped down some breakfast, then searched for Grotbag's bone. Two hours later, it was still nowhere to be seen.

"Don't worry, Grotbag," said Grouchy. "Me and Grunty'll get you a new one! We'll go to the butcher's right now, eh, Grunty?"

Grunty heaved a heavy sigh. "If we *have* to..."

CHAPTER
TWO

The trolls caught the next bus into town
and headed straight to the butcher's.
They were just about to go inside when
they heard a familiar voice.

"No talking, children. And keep in
line!" It was Mr Smart, one of the
teachers from Sparkleton Primary.

The trolls spun round to see Class 3
smiling up at them. They'd "helped out"
in this class before but, oddly, Mr Smart
didn't seem to like them much…

"Hi!" Grunty called, and Grouchy gave
a wave.

"Hello, Mr Trolls," chanted the children.

"We're going to the museum," said
Fred.

"Come with us!" cried Billy and Lottie.

"Oooh, Grunty, *can we*?" squeaked
The Grouch.

Suddenly, Mr Smart marched up.

"No you can't!" he snapped. He glared at Fred, then ushered the children away.

"Oh well," sighed Grouchy. "Never mind. We've got to get Grotbag a bone anyway."

"Yep," said Grunty. "And we will! Just as soon as we've checked out that museum. Mr Smarty-Pants can't stop us, come on!"

He grabbed Grouchy's arm and they raced along the street until they caught up with Class 3. "What are you doing?" cried Mr Smart.

"Who, us?" Grunty shrugged. "Just walking on the pavement! There's no rule that says we can't do that, is there?"

A couple of children sniggered, but Mr Smart glared at the trolls. "Fine!" he snapped. "But just keep out of my way."

They all set off, and soon reached the museum. As the children trooped inside, Mr Smart handed each of them a clipboard and a stack of worksheets. The trolls hurried in behind and followed the class into the Egyptian room.

"Go away!" hissed Mr Smart. "Museums are ... well, quiet places, filled

with priceless treasures. They're not for
noisy trolls like *you*!"

"Who says we're NOISY?" boomed
The Grunt.

"Yeah!" cried Grouchy, giggling. "Come
on, Grunty – let's play Egyptians!"

Cheering, the trolls bounded off to
fiddle with the "priceless treasures". The
children looked on jealously, clutching
their worksheets.

In no time at all, Grunty found a mummy lying in a casket. "Hey, Grouchy, I wonder what's under them bandages?"

"No you don't!" came a voice, as Grouchy reached out a hand. "No touching!" scowled the museum attendant.

He bustled over to Mr Smart. "Keep your *helpers* under control!" he cried.

"No – wait!" blushed Mr Smart. "They're not with me. Honestly!"

The museum attendant shook his head. "I'm warning you!" he said. Then he swept away to polish a sticky vase.

Fuming, Mr Smart marched the trolls into a quiet corner. "*Now* look what you've done!"

"But we didn't do nothing!" Grunty shrugged.

"Just stay here," hissed the teacher. "And … and … *try* to be good!"

No sooner had he stomped away than Grouchy tugged Grunty's waistcoat. "Look," he whispered. "Behind us! Grub!"

Grunty spun round to see a roped-off

area where dummies, dressed as
Egyptians, were sitting around a table
piled with food. "I think it's time for
lunch." He smiled. "Follow me!"

They ducked under the rope and
began tucking into all the
plastic food. "Mmmm,"
said Grouchy, nibbling
a grape.

"Yeah!" burped
Grunty. "Delicious!"
They scoffed a bit
of everything and
were just getting up
to leave when…

"Oi!" yelled an
angry voice. "Not
so fast!"

CHAPTER THREE

The museum attendant hurried over, shaking his fist at the trolls. Grunty spun round, knocking over a cup of fake wine.

"Ooops!" gulped Grouchy. "I'll mop it up." He grabbed a bit of the tablecloth and gave it a sharp tug, sending plates and bowls and plastic food clattering to the floor. CRASH!

The attendant glared at Mr Smart. "Your helpers are out of control! I shall be complaining to your head teacher!"

"Please! No!" wailed Mr Smart. "I've told you, these trolls are nothing to do with me. But I'll clean it up right now. OK, everyone – including you two – OUT!"

He marched everyone out of the room and down a long corridor. At the end of it was a door marked "quiet". He opened it and ushered everyone in.

"This room is for silent working," he hissed. "Now, sit down – ALL of you!" He glowered at the trolls. "Draw something you've seen. NOT the mess!" he added. "I'll be back when I've cleaned it up."

He stormed out, slamming the door, and the children all sat down.

"Mr Smart's so *boring*," groaned Fred. "He never lets us have fun!"

"Yeah," sighed Billy. "Never."

Grunty gazed at the glum-looking children. It wasn't fair ... they deserved some fun. "OK!" he cried. "Forget drawing! Hands up who wants to come exploring instead?"

Grouchy's hand shot up, closely followed by Fred's.

"*Trollific!*" cried Lottie, raising hers too. Soon, everyone's hand was in the air.

"Right," whispered Grunty, opening the door. "Off we go!" They tiptoed down the corridor, past lots of closed doors. "Ancient Rome", it said on one. "The Victorians", it said on another.

Then, suddenly, Grunty stopped. "Check this out!" He pointed at the sign on the door.

DINOSAURS

Strictly NO Entry
– opens at the end of May

"Oh no," grumbled Fred. "If only we'd come next week instead."

"Trust Mr Smart," tutted Billy.

Grunty opened the door and peeped inside. There was nobody around. "Look's like the coast's clear," he whispered. "In you go!"

They hurried inside. The room was filled with enormous dinosaur skeletons. "Wow!" gasped the children. "COOL!"

"OK," sniffed Grunty. "Worksheets out!" Everybody groaned.

"Only joking!" he chuckled. "Let's have some fun!"

THE GRUNT AND THE GROUCH

The children went wild, but not nearly as wild as Grunty and Grouchy! They scaled tails. They slid down necks. They swung from rib to rib! Then everyone played off-ground tag and Grunty and Grouchy were "it". It was the best school trip Class 3 had ever had!

"OK," puffed
Grunty, when everyone had
been tagged. "Time to get back to that
"quiet" room before Mr Smart catches
us!" The children sighed, but hurried out
of the door.

The trolls were just heading after them when Grouchy had a thought. "Hey, Grunty, you know we're meant to be getting a new bone for Grotbag … well, how about one of *these*?"

He pointed at a huge Tyrannosaurus rex, labelled Ty the Terrible.

"Hmmm," said Grunty. "Yeah, why not! I'm sure Ty won't miss one little toe bone!"

Just then, Fred raced back in, followed by Billy and Lottie. "Hey, aren't you two coming?" he cried. "Mr Smart might be back any minute."

"What? Oh, yeah." Grunty smiled. "But first we've got a job to do. Listen up…"

CHAPTER FOUR

Fred gaped at the trolls. "You want a dinosaur bone *for your dog?*"

"That's right!" beamed Grouchy. "And you can help us pull it out!"

"Lottie, you grab the bone, and we'll all hold on to you," said Grunty. "Get a grip everyone! And tug on the count of three."

"O-OK," the children murmured nervously.

"*Don't worry!*" boomed Grunty. "It'll be all right. Ready? One … two … THREE!"

Everyone
pulled on the huge
bone. "Heave!" cried Grunty.

"We are!" puffed the children, tugging
with all their might.

"Oooh!" squealed Grouchy excitedly.
"Here it comes!"

POP! The bone shot out and everyone
toppled backwards, landing in a heap on
the floor. "Good work," beamed Grunty,
grabbing Grotbag's new bone. "Right –
we'd better be getting back. Come on!"

Everyone scrambled to their feet, but
as they hurried to the door they heard a
strange noise. Something right behind
them was … creaking.

Holding their breath, they turned
round. "Uh-oh," Fred muttered. "Look!"

It was Ty the Terrible! He was swaying from side to side and looking *very* unsteady.

"Yikes!" gulped Grouchy. "Run for it! He's going to fa— AARRRGGHH!"

The massive dinosaur toppled to the floor, sending a thick cloud of dust into the air.

CRASH!

As it cleared, Grunty opened his mouth to speak, but no sound came out. There was no doubt about it. They were in BIG trouble.

Grouchy coughed. "Oh well!" he said. "Could have been worse, I suppose."

"What?" squeaked Grunty. "How?"

"Well," said The Grouch, "all the pieces are there! It's just like a big, bony jigsaw. I'm sure we can build him back up again in no time. Come on!"

Ten minutes later, a giant "thing" towered up before them. "See – *perfect*!" Grouchy beamed.

"Well," giggled Lottie, "almost!"

The children hurried out of the door. "We'll be right behind you!" called Grunty. He tucked the toe bone inside his waistcoat. "Better hide this first," he said.

"Good thinking!" nodded Grouchy. "Now let's go."

They darted to the door and pulled

it open. Suddenly, their faces dropped.
Who should be standing on the other
side but ... *Mr Smart!*

Class 3's teacher stepped inside and
peered around the room. "What are you
doing in here?" he hissed.
"And what is THAT?"

He pointed at the
thing behind them.

"It's a ...
*Troll*rannosaurus rex!"
gulped Grunty, scooping
up Grouchy and
legging it.

"Gotta go bone – I
mean – HOME!"
called Grouchy.
"Bye-ee!"

The trolls ran all the way home and
burst in through the front door. "Grotbag!"
panted Grouchy. "Look what we've got
you!"

They watched, open-mouthed, as
their fleabaggy dog trotted brightly
towards them, then dropped something
slobbery at their feet.

"I don't *believe* it!" Grunty growled.
"He's found his old bone. Look!" He
shook his head. "After all that."

He plonked down the dinosaur bone
and Grotbag gave it a sniff, before padding
back to his basket with the old one.

"Never mind!" Grouchy smiled, heaving
Ty's toe bone off the floor. "We could
build our *own* Trollrannosaurus rex! We
just need a few more bones. Do you think

Ty would miss a couple more little ones?"

"What?" groaned Grunty. "Go back to the museum? The only place *I'm* going is back to bed!"

CHAPTER ONE

Whoosh! The Grouch raced into the sitting room. "Look what I've got!" he cried. Grunty, who was reading the newspaper, ignored him.

"Hey, Grunty!" Grouchy prodded his leg. "Don't you want to see?" He waved the matchbox in the air excitedly.

The Grunt looked up. "Oi!" he cried. "That's … that's … *mine!* How many times have I told you, stop meddling with my stuff!"

"But they don't *like* being cooped up," muttered Grouchy, sliding the lid off the box. Hundreds of fleas sprang into the air.

"*Grouchy!*" yelled Grunty. "NOOOO!"

Suddenly, there came a knock at the door.

"Oh *no!*" snapped The Grunt. "Now we've got a visitor too!"

He stomped to the door and tugged it open. The postman stood on the doormat, holding a parcel and wearing a big smile.

"Hello!" he said brightly. "Lovely day! Here's a par—"

But before he could finish, Grunty snatched it off him and slammed the door in his face.

"Oooh, Grunty!" squealed Grouchy, bouncing up and down. "Let's see!" He tugged at Grunty's waistcoat.

"No you don't!" said The Grunt. "*You* need to go and round up those fleas."

"But I'll do it *later*," Grouchy wailed. "I promise."

Grunty tutted and hurried over to the sofa. He popped the parcel down and tore off its brown paper wrapping. "Oh, *look*!" cried Grouchy. "That's a flashy box!"

He watched as Grunty opened its lid, then they both peered inside.

"*Wow!*" gasped The Grunt. "A racing car!" He lifted out the shiny red car. "Oh, boy!" he cried, eyes twinkling. "I'm gonna have fun with *you*."

"Me too!" beamed Grouchy, climbing on to the sofa to get a closer look. His fingers closed around the car, but Grunty held on tight.

Let go!

No, you let go!

An hour passed, but the trolls were still there. Neither of them would let go of the car, though they both needed the toilet.

"OK," growled Grunty desperately. "Let's put the car on the sofa and *neither* of us will play with it!"

"Errrrrr…" muttered Grouchy, jigging about. "*OK!*"

They put it down and raced to the bathroom. Grouchy got there first and zipped inside.

"Hurry up!" yelled The Grunt, hopping from foot to foot. "And *don't* touch a single thing of mine. DO YOU HEAR ME?"

He paced up and down the landing

until Grouchy trotted back out. Rolled up in his hand was Grunty's *Mega-Monster-Mag!*

"*Hey!*" boomed the big purple troll. "That's *mine!*" He made a grab for it as he darted to the loo, but Grouchy swiftly dodged out of the way.

Two minutes later, the bathroom door opened and Grunty thumped back out. Grouchy was sitting at the top of the stairs, reading a *Grime-Time Tale* and wearing the free "Splatman" mask he'd ripped off the comic's cover.

Gritting his teeth, Grunty thundered towards him and tore off the sticky green mask.

"Oi!" squeaked Grouchy. "*Give that back!* I lend you *my* stuff all the time!"

"No, you don't."

"Yes, I do."

"Don't."

"Do."

"DON'T!" yelled Grunty. "And I've had enough of you ALWAYS taking mine!"

He stomped into the bedroom, a fiery glint in his eyes.

"From now on things round here are going to change."

CHAPTER TWO

Grouchy crept across the landing and peeped round the bedroom door. Grunty was flinging pillows off the beds.

After a while, he trudged back out with a pile of filthy blankets. "Right," he growled, spotting The Grouch. "Follow me!"

He thumped downstairs. Grouchy trailed behind. "*What's going on?*" he wailed.

Grunty gave an angry snort. "You'll see!"

When they reached the sitting room,
he dumped the blankets down. "Now go
and fetch *all* your stuff!" snapped
Grunty. "And I'll fetch all mine. You put
yours on *that* side of the room," he
pointed a fat, hairy finger, "and I'll put
mine on *this* side!"

Grouchy gave a nod and trotted off.

In no time at all, two grotty piles of
stuff sat on opposite sides of the room.
"Right, what's next?" muttered The
Grunt. "Ah, yes!"

He marched to a drawer, opened it
and took out a hammer and some nails.
"This'll teach you!" he chuckled to
himself.

Picking up one of the blankets,
Grunty climbed on to a chair.

"*Grunty!*" shrieked Grouchy. "What are you *doing*?"

Grunty didn't answer. He lifted the blanket to the ceiling, shoved a nail through one of its corners, then raised the hammer and whacked it in hard…

BANG, BANG, BANG!

One by one, the grimy blankets were hammered into the ceiling, where they hung down like a woolly wall, splitting the room exactly in half.

"There!" said Grunty, getting down off the chair on his side of the wall. He could hear The Grouch shuffling about on the other side.

Grunty gave a satisfied nod. Now half the telly, the sofa and the racing car were on *his* side of the room, and the other halves were on the other side … with *Grouchy*!

"Ha!" Grunty smiled, prodding the blanket-wall. "No nicking *my* stuff any more! Now stay over there for *ever*! Do you hear?"

"*Fine!*" cried Grouchy. "Suits me!"

He flumped down on his side of the sofa and Grunty flumped down on his, each wondering what the other was up to…

They sat there for *ages*. It was awfully quiet. Grunty gazed at his bit of car sitting on the sofa beside him. He edged it towards him a tiny bit. Grouchy edged it back. "Uh-uh!" he tutted.

Twiddling their thumbs, they both stared into space, trying to decide what to do. Finally, Grouchy switched on the telly and started to watch half a football match. Grunty began watching the other half on his side…

Grotville Rovers, their favourite team, was playing Angel United and, for *once*, Grotville was winning.

"Come on, you Grots!" Grunty heard Grouchy chant when the ball was booted over into his side.

"Hey, Grouchy!" he called, leaping up. "What's happening?"

"*Oooh!*" gasped Grouchy. "*Ahhh! Wow!*"

"WHAT'S GOING ON?" yelled Grunty. He stomped across to the telly and started dragging it over to his side.

"Give me back my half of the telly!" Grouchy yelled.

He flew at the screen and clung on tight, but Grunty was too strong. "Right then!" Grouchy puffed. "You've asked for this…"

He reached down and pushed a button. Suddenly, the screen went black. "*Hey!*" boomed Grunty. "*What did you do that for?*"

"Serves you right!" giggled Grouchy. "Serves you right!"

CHAPTER THREE

As they flumped back down on the sofa,
the car caught Grouchy's eye. He edged it
to his side. Grunty edged it back. "Uh-uh!"

They folded their arms. "Hey, Grunty,"
called Grouchy, "what are you doing right
now?"

"Um…" yawned Grunty. "I'm sitting –
no, wait … I'm … I'm building a
supersonic rocket!"

He strolled across to his pile of stuff
and snatched up a filthy saucepan.

Then he started to whack it hard with a wooden spoon.

"*Phew!*" he puffed. "Rocket-building's hard work! But soon I'll be off to the moon! I wonder if it's made of mouldy cheese…"

It was quiet for a moment. Then, "Can I come with you?" Grouchy called.

"Certainly not!" sniffed The Grunt.

"That's not very friendly!" muttered Grouchy.

"Well, we're *not* friends, are we!" Grunty banged the pan again. "Wow – this rocket's coming on a treat!"

Suddenly, a small green face peeped under the blanket-wall. "Oi!" yelled Grunty. "Stop *spying* on me!"

"Ha ha!" giggled Grouchy, pointing a finger. "Your rocket's just a pan!"

Grunty threw down the saucepan and glowered. "Get back over to *your* side!" he bellowed, marching up to the blankets. Grouchy's head disappeared as he howled with laughter. "Hee hee!"

They sat back down on their bits of sofa and no one spoke for ten minutes. Then Grunty's tummy gave a giant rumble.

He gazed around, delighted to see that the door to the kitchen was on *his* side! Licking his hairy lips, he leaped up and thundered over.

"Grunty?" came a little voice.

"Where are you going?"

Grunty didn't reply. He already had his head in the fridge and was eyeing up the mouldy food. "Mmmm…" he dribbled greedily. "All for me!"

Chuckling to himself, he trooped back with a huge chunk of plughole-hair pie. He sat himself down and began munching noisily.

"What are you eating?" Grouchy called.

Grunty gave a burp. "None of your business."

The Grouch frowned. There was *nothing* to do and Grunty had all the food! If only that parcel hadn't arrived, they'd probably still be friends. "Silly car!" he muttered to himself.

He glared at the box on the arm of the sofa then nudged it over the edge. As it hit the floor, something tumbled out…

Grouchy picked it up and examined it. It looked a bit like a TV remote control, but had four little buttons labelled "forward", "back", "left" and "right", and a long bouncy wire at the top.

Suddenly, a grin spread across Grouchy's face as he worked out what it was. "The remote control for the *racing car*!" he whispered, and a plan began to form in his head. This could be *just* the thing he needed…

"Grunty," he called a few moments later. "I need a snack – I'm *starving*! Tell you what, if you give me some grub, I'll let *you* have the car!"

"Huh?" grunted Grunty. "You'll give me the car?"

"*Absolutely!*" cried The Grouch, hiding the remote control under his hat.

"Well ... um ... yeah, OK!" called Grunty. "*Deal!*"

He lifted a blanket, tossed some pie underneath, then grabbed hold of the car. "Right!" he cried. "I'm off to do some racing in the garden!"

Grouchy snatched up the pie and sniggered. "Wait for me!" he called. He lowered his voice. "This is gonna be *trollific!*"

CHAPTER FOUR

The Grunt hurried into the garden and
Grouchy raced behind, gobbling down
the chunk of plughole-hair pie.

Grunty placed the car on the cracked
path alongside a nice clump of weeds.

"Oooh, great!" cried Grouchy. "The
perfect track for me – I mean you – to
race the car on!"

"Right!" Grunty nodded. "Here I g—"

"Wait a minute!" cried The Grouch.
"You need a flag to start you off. And, as

I'm just *watching*, I could wave it for you!"

Grunty smiled. "Oh, good idea!"

He pulled out a snotty hanky and handed it to Grouchy. The Grouch licked off the bogeys and beamed.

"I'll just climb up that tree," he said. "To get a good view."

"OK, but hurry up!" Grunty cried.

Grouchy climbed to the top of the tree. Then, when The Grunt wasn't looking, he whisked the remote from underneath his hat and tucked it under the hanky.

"OK!" he called. "Ready?"

"Ready!" Grunty replied.

"On your marks … get set … go!"
Grouchy waved the hanky in the air and
pressed the forward button on the
remote. *Dzzzzzzzzz* went the little car,
shooting off down the path.

Grunty gaped. "Huh?" he shrugged.
He lumbered off after it, as Grouchy
pressed the buttons wildly.

The car veered off the
garden path and
started to zoom
round the pond.

"What's going
on?" panted
Grunty. "Come …
back … here!"

"*Vrrrooooom!*" giggled Grouchy from the top of his tree. He leaned forward to get a better view and accidentally pressed the "left" button. BANG! The car smacked into the fence at full speed.

"*Bother!*" whispered Grouchy, climbing down from the tree and racing over. The car was upside-down in the nettles, and missing three wheels and a bumper. Grouchy shook his head. "Uh-oh."

Grunty puffed over. "Oh no!" he cried. "What's *wrong* with that stupid car?"

Grouchy shot the remote behind his back. "Dunno."

Just then, a titchy peep-squeak boy
popped his head over the fence. "DAD!"
he wailed. "*Look!* They've wrecked my car!"

Mr Busybody, the trolls' next-door
neighbour, marched up shaking with
rage. "Oi!" he bellowed. "That's *our* car!"

"It's not," cried Grunty. "It's MINE!
The postman brought it, didn't he
Grouchy?"

"Actually, I think it's *mine*,"
Grouchy muttered.

"It's not EITHER of
yours!" yelled Mr
Busybody. "YOU
were just
meant to look
after it until WE
got back home.

The postman left us a note – see! We were just coming round to get it."

Grunty and Grouchy stared at each other. Neither had checked the name on the parcel before Grunty had ripped off the wrapping.

"Right," hissed Mr Busybody. "Hand it over!"

Grunty scooped up what was left of the car and passed it across, and Grouchy lobbed over the remote control when Grunty wasn't looking.

"We don't want it anyway," sniffed Grunty. "Got a mind of its own, that car!"

"Yeah," nodded Grouchy. "*Troll* games are better! That car's only made us fight. Come on, Grunty – let's go and play the windy-pop game instead."

Grunty smiled. "Hmmm, good idea!"
The trolls linked arms and were about
to go inside when – *swoosh!* – a bright red
dragon kite appeared in the sky. It soared
down into their garden and landed in the
thistles.

"*Wow!*" gasped Grunty.

"*Wow!*" giggled Grouchy.

MINE!